Doris Bean
and The Queen

Martin
Waddell

Illustrated by
Scoular Anderson

•••• dingles&company

First published in the United States of America in 2008 by
dingles & company
P.O. Box 508
Sea Girt, New Jersey 08750

First Printing

Website: www.dingles.com
E-mail: info@dingles.com

Library of Congress Catalog Card Number
2007906337

ISBN
978-1-59646-964-8 (library binding)
978-1-59646-965-5 (paperback)

Doris Bean and the Queen
Text © Martin Waddell, 2002
This U.S. edition of *Doris Bean and the Queen*, originally published
in English in 2007, is published by arrangement with
Oxford University Press.

Printed in China

Contents

3 Orley Cottages
Cowhill
Thursday 5th August

Dear Queen,

I think you've been working too hard and you need a day off from your duties.

If you can get away, please visit me and we could play games in my garden.

Yours sincerely,

Your friend,

DorisBean

Chapter 1

The Queen Up a Tree

One day, Doris Bean wrote to the Queen.

The next day, Doris got tea ready and sat around for ages. But the Queen didn't come. So Doris went to check her Garden Worm Watch, instead. She was counting worms beneath the big tree in the garden, when ...

"Psst! Doris," someone hissed from the tree. "I've just escaped from my footman and butler. Is it safe to come down?"

It was the Queen.

"There's only me here, Queen," said Doris.

"Yippee! Let's play!" shouted the Queen. She hopped down from the tree, so she could play games with Doris.

They played Tag
and Hide and Seek
and I-am-the-Queen-of-the-Castle.
(This was one the Queen knew very
well.)

"Hopscotch next!" cried the Queen.
She hadn't played hopscotch for ages,
except by herself in her room, all
alone. No one plays hopscotch with
queens.

Then ...

Right through the hedge came a
tank. Out of the tank jumped the
Queen's footman and butler.

(The one looking angry is the butler.
The one with the wig is the footman.)

"Gotcha, Ma'am!" cried the butler, grabbing the Queen.

"Save me, Doris!" the Queen cried, but the footman was too fast.

He grabbed Doris. He slipped a ball and chain on her leg, so she couldn't move.

"You're a very bold Queen. You've really upset the Queen Mother, running off," the Queen's butler scolded. "You're coming home with us, right this minute!"

"Will not!" said the Queen, stamping her foot. "I've only been free for an hour."

But the butler grabbed one end of the Queen ...

... and the footman took the other,
and they carried the Queen back to the
tank.

The Queen kicked
and shouted
and struggled
and wriggled ...
but she had to go back in the tank.
Doris couldn't help. She was busy
sawing the ball and chain off her leg.

"We'll be watching you, Doris Bean!" the footman and the butler shouted.

Then the tank went back through the hole it had made in Doris' hedge.

A piece of paper flew out of the tank. It was a note from the Queen.

That's when Doris knew she was in for an adventure!

Chapter 2

The Royal Escape Plan

Doris dropped the ball and chain.

Then she ran over and picked up the Queen's note. It was written on royal note paper.

MEMO

FROM: H M THE QUEEN

TO: DORIS BEAN

SUBJECT: My Royal Escape Plan

Dear Doris,

Come to my castle at sunrise.
Whistle three times. Bring a rope
and a two-seater bike and a disguise
to fit a medium-sized queen.

Yours secretly
Your royal friend,

The Queen

The next morning, before dawn, Doris crept to the castle.

She'd hidden the bike in the hedge.

Doris whistled, "God Save the Queen" three times very softly, just as the sun rose.

A window opened high up, and out looked the Queen.

"Toss the rope up, Doris. I want to get down!" hissed the Queen.

Doris had brought her toy bow and arrow with her.

She tied the rope to the arrow. There was a suction cup on the end of the arrow. Doris knew that the arrow would stick to the wall. Then the Queen could slide down the rope.

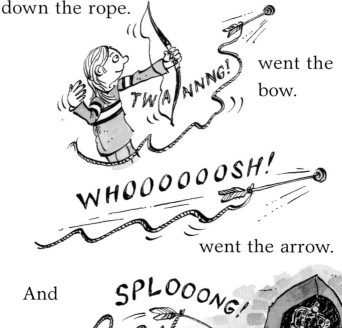

went the bow.

went the arrow.

And

It stuck to the wall near the window.

"Well done, Doris!" cried the Queen, hitching up her pajamas.

The Queen slid down the rope. But the arrow gave way and ...

The poor Queen was dumped in the moat.

The Queen's golden pajamas got wet, but she wasn't hurt. She could swim like a fish. All queens learn to swim when they're on their yachts.

"Let's go!" cried the Queen, bouncing out of the moat.

"Where to?" asked Doris.

"To the seaside!" cried the Queen. "I haven't played there for ages."

They jumped on the bike and tore off down the street.

The Queen had long legs, so she worked the pedals.

"Remember to stop at the stop sign, Queen!" Doris shouted.

Doris dinged the bell to warn people
that their Queen was coming.
Ding! Ding! Ding! DING!

SCREEEEEEEEEEECH!

"Wow!" cried Doris, looking behind her, but the Queen pedaled furiously on.

The Queen and Doris dumped their bike at the back of the train station.

"Oh well," Doris mumbled, "at least no one got hurt!"

Doris bought two round-trip tickets
(Super Saver) to the seaside.

The Queen changed into her
disguise. Doris had brought her a pair
of black jeans (medium-size) and a top.
She had also brought a flashy pair of
sunglasses with butterfly wings.

They got on the train.

"Does my disguise work?" asked the
Queen.

"Take the crown off, Queen," Doris
advised.

The Queen put her crown on the
seat beside her.

When they got off the train, the
Queen was very excited.

She saw the sea and wanted to play
at once. So they ran down to the beach
and played tag with the waves.

They made sandcastles. They fished for crabs in the rock pools, and then they walked on the sand for what seemed likes ages and ages.

Then ...

"Queen," Doris asked. "Where's your crown?"

"Oh, golly," the Queen gasped.
She had left her crown on the train.

Someone had spotted it and got on the phone with the butler.

He searched the palace, but there was no sign of the Queen.

Then he found Doris' footprints down by the moat, and Doris' rope, and her arrow.

"Doris Bean's been at it again. She's stolen the Queen," sighed the butler.

And he ordered the police to start hunting for the Queen and Doris.

Chapter 3

The Hunt for Doris

"Look! Now I've done it!" said Doris.
They'd come up to the shop to buy an
ice-cream. And that is where Doris
saw the newspaper.

DORIS BEAN STEALS QUEEN!

HUNT FOR MISSING MONARCH!

Doris was upset. Police were
running all over the place searching
for the Queen. What would happen
when they found her?

One thing was for sure.

They were going to be very angry with Doris.

The Queen looked worried. But she was really quite pleased by the fuss.

"One likes to know one is missed," she murmured to Doris.

"You'd better call home, Queen. Tell them I haven't stolen you," Doris suggested. But the Queen wasn't listening.

She'd seen the fair.

The Queen tried to walk in without paying, as queens usually do. But the man told her she had to line up with everyone else.

The Queen was really cross, until Doris told her what a line was. Then she was pleased.

The Queen liked meeting her people, and there were lots of them in the line. She gossiped a lot with old ladies.

"What shall we do first?" asked the Queen.

"Give ourselves up," said poor Doris. But the Queen was heading off for the speedboats.

Doris got drenched. So did the Queen.

They slid down the slippery slide.

Doris ended up in a pile under the Queen.

"Now for this one!" cried the Queen.

She dragged Doris onto the Spooky Ghost Train.

"YAAAAA," yelled the Queen. "OOO OOOOOH," the Queen shuddered and shook.

"AAAAAAAAAAA!" screamed the Queen.

"Let's do that again!" said the Queen. "One just *adores* being scared!"

"Call home NOW, Queen," Doris pleaded.

"Not till one's finished one's fun!" said the Queen. She had just seen the bumper cars.

"Oh, no, Ma'am!" gasped Doris. (She remembered the bicycle ride.)

She was too late.

The Queen grabbed the steering wheel of the red car. It was number thirteen.

"Buzz off, lady! You've busted my car!" the man told the Queen, when she climbed from the wreckage.

"Don't you dare be rude to your Queen!" said the Queen.

The bumper car man took a close look at the Queen. He lifted her glasses off her nose. He knew it was her. And he ran off to find the police.

"Run, Queen!" Doris yelled. "Run, or they'll catch us!"

They got away from the fair, but there were police everywhere.

They were all looking at pictures of Doris.

"I need a disguise," Doris decided.

Chapter 4

The Queen on the Run

Doris bought a huge Mexican hat. She pulled it down over her ears. Now, no one could see she was Doris.

Even the Queen didn't know Doris was Doris, until the hat stopped beside her and spoke. "Don't tell anyone else you are Queen, Queen. Even if they *are* rude," Doris whispered. "We're on the run. We've got to be careful."

They went into the movies. It was a good place to hide. It was dark inside, and no one could see them.

But when they came out, a policeman was asking everyone questions.

He saw a lady in butterfly glasses with a small someone all covered up in a very big hat ... and something about them made him suspicious.

"Beg your pardon, madam, have you seen our Queen?" the policeman asked.

"Yes, I have," said the lady, quick as a flash. "She went that way on a horse, with a girl who was wearing a hat. The hat looked just like the one that my friend is wearing."

"If I catch Doris, we'll split the reward," cried the policeman. He ran off, blowing his whistle like mad.

Then he stopped whistle blowing and stood still, looking puzzled. He thought about what the lady had said – and what had made him suspicious.

The policeman whirled right around. He ran back, shouting, "Stop, Queen and Doris! You're nicked!"

By this time, the Queen and Doris were far, far away.

They were running like mad. They dodged this way ...

... and this way ...

... and that.

"Oh, pardon me!" said the Queen. And this way and that ...

... through the crowd.

"Phew! That was close!" breathed
the Queen, diving into a bus shelter.
Then she hid behind Doris' hat,
hoping she wouldn't be seen.

"We're sunk this time, Queen,"
Doris cried. She was looking at the
poster stuck up on the wall.

"Oh, no!" Doris groaned. "Now I'll
go to prison for stealing the Queen."

Chapter 5

"What Does One Do Now?"

They stayed in the bus shelter.

Doris was afraid to go out, in case she was arrested.

The Queen wasn't much use.

She kept asking, "What does one do now, Doris?"

"I don't know," said Doris. "I'm just about to get arrested."

The Queen thought for a bit. She saw Doris was scared. She wanted to help her.

Then the Queen's face brightened
up.

"I *am* the Queen, Doris!" she said.
"Queens tell people what to do."

"Stop boasting, Queen!"
Doris moped. "I know
that already."

"There are some good things about
being Queen," said the Queen.

"Like what, Queen?" asked Doris.

"Like ... I'm the boss of all the police, and I own all the prisons!" the Queen said. "That's what queens are for. It comes with the job. The police can't arrest me. I'll just tell them you didn't steal me. No one will argue, because I am the Queen, after all."

"That's all right then," said Doris. "But we ought to go home, before things get worse."

"Don't want to!" pouted the Queen.

"My mom will be angry!" Doris said. "I'm not supposed to go stealing queens."

"Well, okay, Doris!" sighed the Queen. "I'll explain to your mom. I'll call for my car and we'll go home, right now."

And she did, from a telephone outside the post office. Doris kept watch, in case any police came by.

And so Doris rode home in the royal Rolls Royce with the Queen.

Everyone cheered as they drove up to Doris' house.

Then Doris popped out, straight into the arms of her mom.

Next day, a top secret note came for Doris. It was hidden inside a cake from the Queen.

TOP SECRET NOTE
For D. Bean's eyes only

Dear Doris,
One demands to be stolen again. Please arrange it soon.

Yours sincerely.
Your royal friend
The Queen

Now they slip out once a week,
using brand new disguises.

Which one is Doris? Which one is
the Queen?

About the author

I was answering letters sent to me by a school. A little girl wanted to know if I would like to come to visit her at her house. Suppose she'd started her letter "Dear Queen" instead of "Dear Martin Waddell"? What might the letter have said?

That kind of supposing often gives me the start of a story ... as it did with Doris Bean.